I0520088

Folding Reality

By Mit Sandru

Chivileri Publishing

ISBN 0983669546

101821

2

Table of Contents

Chapter 1. Weird

I unfold the map and look up. Dunes of yellow-beige sand open before my eyes. They go on forever. The sky is deep blue, without a cloud. It looks like the Sahara. How did I get here, in the middle of this desert?

From my left, two Bedouins approach, pushing a lawn mower – a gasoline-powered, red lawn mower. There's no greenery anywhere in sight. What are they going to mow? Sand? They ignore me and my open mouth, and continue on their way.

A dogsled appears in the distance, raising clouds of dust. As it gets closer, I can see that it resembles an Alaskan sled, led by a team of twelve Malamutes. Cute – each dog wears sunglasses. Considering the brilliant sun and the dogs' blue eyes, that seems very practical. The dogs are pulling in earnest, their purple tongues flopping out of their open mouths, blowing condensation as if they were in subzero weather. A woman clad in a black burkha rides on the back rails. An Arab man dressed in a dark, pinstriped suit sits in the sled with his arms folded. He has a short, trimmed beard, his hair is sleekly combed back, and he wears mirrored sunglasses. He looks at me over the rim of his sunglasses as he's passing by. I wonder; should I wave at him, at them? The woman – the wind blowing her burkha against her voluptuous curves – pays no attention to me. And before I know it, they've disappeared in the desert, leaving just the sled's trail in the sand. And the dust, of course.

I must be dreaming. I look for the map, but it is gone. The wind blew it away, I think. I must have been so spellbound by the sled riding on the sand that I let it go. I've surely dozed off in my chair, in my office. I pinch myself. I am awake and fully aware. Could what I saw be a mirage? I think not. It was darn real.

I hear people chattering behind me. I turn and see a small crowd in front of some sort of attraction, like the kind in an amusement park tent. Except this is a Bedouin tent. Now, what could this be? The people waiting in line to enter whatever is there seem to be very excited about what they'll be seeing. I get in line, too. Try everything at least once, I tell myself.

We enter a small room inside the tent. The guide, a shapely young woman dressed in a baby-blue uniform, gives instructions: "You must say 'I-O-W' loudly before entering through the shroud. Do not enter before you chant 'I-O-W'."

The walls of the square room turn blue, indigo blue, as if the walls were projection screens lit from the outside. Strange golden symbols like Egyptian hieroglyphs appear in a grid pattern on the walls. In front of us is the shroud. Actually it's a canvas, a gray and dingy-looking drape, which must be pulled up to enter underneath to see whatever is to be seen behind it. The group starts, "I – "

Screw this! I can't wait for this charade! I spring forward, pull up the drape, which is more like a tarp, bend down, and sneak in.

Suddenly, I'm outside. The colors are bright. I'm standing on fine yellow sand. Through the air miniature shimmering clouds – no, not clouds, but small clusters of insects – fly by. But they're not insects, either, and some of them fall to the ground. They're colorful balls, bigger than marbles, about an inch in diameter. They bounce as they land. One of them, clear as glass, lands near my feet. I pick it up to inspect it.

It's made of solid glass and not plastic, as I thought. These things could kill you if one lands on your head. And they fly fast, as if they're being fired from a large shotgun. The group behind the tarp curtain finishes their chant and rushes into this strange setting – dangerous, too.

"Watch out for those flying balls!" I yell to warn them. More of the balls fall on the sand, bouncing like golf balls, sparkling like ice. Could these be hail, pebbles of ice? They sure look like hail on the sand. No, the ball I still hold in my hand is warm, not cold. It's glass. But why are they flying in those clusters, like miniature clouds, just a few feet above our heads? The people around me pay no attention to my warning. They jump with joy with their hands up, some twirling. Blue, red, green, purple, and transparent balls drop all around us. Are the others seeing something different than what I'm seeing?

I'm not going to hang around this place. Any one of us could be seriously hurt or killed. I run back to the curtain, pull it up, and get back into the indigo-blue room with the golden symbols. There's a new group of people in the room. There are no exits other than the canvas-shroud. The people chant, "I-O-W." And they rush, lifting the canvas and passing underneath it to the outside. I follow, staying close to the curtain this time.

The small clouds of flying glass balls are no more. At least now it's safe from getting bonked on the head from them! The sand is gone; the ground is now made up of square mirrored tiles, a reflective surface that reminds me of a frozen lake. I step on it carefully, hoping it will not crack. It's solid. It's strange to see my reflection below.

Even stranger, just nearby, there's a line of gharials. I know they're gharials by their long, narrow jaws, with rows of teeth along the sides. They're lined up, one after the other, as if they're in a parade, although none of them move.

"Beware of the crocodile," a woman says, pointing at a dark blue-gray creature.

"It's a gharial," I say.

"Beware of the alligator," says a boy, and he jumps over one. That gharial raises its head and snaps its jaws, making a sound like a clasp closing on a purse.

There's nothing to see here, other than the animals and the mirrored floor. Again, I must be missing something here. Those people are seeing something I'm not, I think to myself. As I walk back cautiously, turning around, watching for other dangers, every so often checking on the gharials as well, something knocks against my leg. I jump. It's a statue of an owl. I kick it and it bounces away, making the hollow sound of a tin can.

From its open bottom glass balls, just like the ones I saw previously, pour out, littering the smooth mirrored floor. This is treacherous to walk on – step on a ball, and you'll find yourself rolling on them and falling on your back. The gharials turn, opening their jaws as they advance toward me.

Screw this! I run back through the curtain, back into the indigo-blue room. It's empty now. Only the attending girl, dressed in her baby-blue uniform, is in there, leaning against the wall.

"What is this madness?" I shout.

"Did you chant I-O-W?"

"What? No. What for? The other people shouted the letters," I reply.

"You must chant I-O-W."

"How do I get out of here?"

"The only way out is through the shroud." She points at it with her well-manicured index finger.

"No way! I'm not going out there again. Where is the exit?"

She keeps pointing at the shroud.

I'm about to lose my temper. Should I scream for help? No. I'm a grown man; I can figure this out. "Why say those letters? What do they mean?"

She smiles. "They stand for 'I Often Wonder'."

"'I Often Wonder' what?"

"That's what you'll have to see for yourself."

"OK, OK! I-O-W." I turn reluctantly to the shroud, and I see that it's now made of a light material, perhaps silk. I lift it and go under cautiously, expecting to see open jaws.

I exit into a gleaming metal tunnel. I've never seen anything like this before. It's space age and beyond. The tunnel extends so far that its end looks like a dot, and it's rotating clockwise. A map flutters on the curved floor as it slides due to the rotation. I step inside the massive tube, leaning and stepping to the right to compensate for the spinning. I pick up the map, unfold it, and find myself back in my office, in my chair.

Was I tripping on something? I don't take drugs, so what did I just experience? It felt real, not like a dream or a hallucination. The map is still in my hand. It's a map of Orange County. Is the map cursed? Maybe it was the act of folding and unfolding it?

What's going on?

My eyes fall on the calendar on the wall. It was folded before I pinned it there. With trembling hands, I pull the tacks out and hold the calendar at arm's length, afraid it might bite me. Was it the act of folding or unfolding the map that sent me elsewhere? Or was it the map itself? How about this calendar? It drops on my desk, and it folds along its original creases, and

. . .

Chapter 2. Purgatory

I find myself in a narrow, crooked street surrounded by crudely made mud and limestone walls. Some portions of the pavement are made from the same yellowish limestone, but most of the street is hard packed dirt. It seems as though rain hasn't visited this place in a while.

I'm dressed in a robe made of some rough, scratchy gray cloth. A rope around my waist serves as a belt. My feet are dusty, and I'm wearing leather sandals with wooden soles. I don't think that I'm wearing any underwear – actually, I'm sure I'm not. I touch my head and realize that I'm wearing a turban. I'm a towelhead? Am I in the Middle East somewhere? That explains the dusty smell and the beyond-medieval architecture.

I turn around, trying to get my bearings. Since I don't know where I am, it doesn't matter where I go, so I walk, keeping in the shade of the walls. I pass heavy wooden doors that access the houses that must be behind these walls. At times I smell smoke and the aroma of food, other times I smell dung and excrement, and occasionally jasmine flowers.

At the intersection of an adjacent street, I see a temple above tall, crenellated stone walls up the hill. Something looks familiar about this temple. Could it be? It looks almost like the Second Temple in Jerusalem, from what I remember from history books. As I advance, the streets become completely paved with stones, and the walls are better made. I walk, stumbling in awe. There are more, many more people in the streets by now. Beggars abound, displaying gross deformities. There's a stench of urine, and I have to be careful not to step in a freshly laid donkey pie.

These streets don't seem to have any rhyme or reason in their layout, and, at times, I have to backtrack to get nearer to the walls of the Temple Mount. I'm sure that's what I see ahead of me. I'm so mesmerized by what I see that I don't even bother to ask myself how I got there. After my previous experience, I'm questioning less the how and more the why.

There's a plume of smoke rising from behind the tall walls, and there seems to be much commotion over there at the temple. I stop, place my hands on my hips, and contemplate where my calendar folding has brought me.

From around the nearest corner, I'm rammed by a bearded man running like he's being chased by bulls. We both tumble down, and I'm about to give him a piece of my mind and tell him to watch where's he's going, when he gets up. Without paying any attention to me, he takes off, leaving behind his sack. Being of a decent upbringing, I pick up his sack – which is heavy and full of clanking objects – and run after him, shouting at him to stop and come get his sack. I'm slower than he is, what with the weight of the sack I'm hauling, and I soon lose him down the crooked, narrow streets.

I stop, panting and wondering what's going on. Behind me, a mob is running my way. They look angry, and some of them are brandishing sticks. I take a better look and see they're soldiers with sharp spears, determined to skewer someone. Dogs run ahead of them, barking menacingly. I better get out of their way. But I can't find any side streets to disappear down, and I run into a dead end.

The mob catches up with me and slowly advances. The dogs charge at me. To defend myself, I swing the sack at them. Whatever's in that sack is heavy enough to knock two of the dogs down, and they run away, yelping, while the others bark from a respectful distance. One or two aren't deterred; they bite into the sack, with me pulling at one end and the angry dogs tearing it apart at the other.

To my surprise, shiny metal objects – pots, plates, and candleholders – spill out of the sack, banging onto the stone ground. I can't believe my eyes. Is that gold, or mere bronze? I don't have much time to inspect them before I'm knocked over the head with a rod.

I wake up in a dark, damp, and awfully bad-smelling place, lying on cold stones. My head – I'm not even sure if I have a head anymore – is hurting beyond belief. I feel a throbbing bump right behind my left ear and dried blood around it. The whole place is spinning. I black out again.

When I wake up, two guys are dragging me by my feet. My head bumps on the stones of the corridor, but that's bearable compared to when they drag me up the stairs. Every step illuminates a new constellation in my head. I end up in a courtyard, or maybe it's the bottom of a pit. The outside sunlight sends jolts of electricity through my brain. I close my eyes, hoping something favorable will now be done about my situation.

It is, but it isn't favorable. I'm disrobed, now butt naked, and my hands are tied with leather straps to an iron ring on the wall. I have to stand on my toes, because the bastards tied me up too high. From above I hear people talking about me. Although I understand the words, they don't exactly sound like English. Could they be Aramaic or Hebrew? I've never known these languages, but I do now.

I listen some more, and I get it. They've confused me with a thief. The bronze wares in the sack were stolen. The guy who ran over me was the thief, and I was caught holding the bag.

"Gentlemen! Up there!" I shout. "I'm not the guy you're looking for. I am not a thief!"

They respond with laughter. "We don't need any defense or confession from you," one of them says. "As far as we're concerned, you're guilty."

"Wait, wait, you're making a big mistake. I am an honest and law-abiding citizen."

"Not honest and not a Roman citizen."

"I'm telling you the truth, so help me, God."

"You'd better pray to a strong God, because – "

"Why the hell are you deliberating with that criminal, Horatio?" interrupts another man, this time speaking Latin.

"We were having fun, *judex*," says Horatio in Latin, which I also can understand. "He is somehow well-spoken, but a Jew, nevertheless."

I speak to the judge in Latin: "Your honor, it is such a pleasure to see you arrive. I was trying to explain that I'm not a thief or the thief you are seek – "

A line of fire crosses my back. The fucking judge gave the order, and the flogging begins. I scream at the top of my lungs after the second lash, and the pain goes all the way down to the bottom of my feet. I don't remember anything after the third lash.

I wake up in the dark and make the mistake of trying to move – I faint again. I wake up later but don't try to move this time. I have thin skin, and I'm delirious with pain. I touch my back tenderly; it feels like raw meat. Fuck! What did I do to deserve this?

Someone grabs me by the feet. "Hold it!" I scream. "Don't drag me!" They drag me anyway. They take me to another pit, which must be the sentencing pit. I don't remember what they say, nor do I defend myself. I must have fainted during the sentencing, because I wake up in the dark again. I get no food or water, and I'm burning with fever.

I'm short of breath, my back is on fire, and my left palm and arm hurt like crazy. What in hell? A big nail the size of a spike is impaled into my palm. My arm is stretched out, and rough ropes tie my arm at the elbow to a wood beam. What's the meaning of this?

I can't believe what I see when I look down. I'm on a pole of some kind, and my feet are nailed to the pole. I can't feel them. They're

21

overlapped and pinned to the pole with an even larger spike, a railroad spike. I can't breathe. I inhale deeply, gasping for air.

I'm afraid to look at my right arm, which I don't feel at all, but I must. My right arm is wrapped with a rope to the beam just like the left arm, and a nail head protrudes from my right palm as well.

I'm being crucified?

"Jesus!" I shout to the sky.

"Who?"

I hear a voice from my right. Another man, in a terrible state, with rags for his clothes, is crucified, just like me. Farther away, there is another poor soul on another cross. Actually, they're not crosses, but large Ts.

"What's going on?" I ask, even though I'm afraid of the answer.

"We're crucified," says the man near me.

For crying out loud, I'm being crucified on Golgotha – next to Jesus? I just folded a calendar for Christ's sake! That's all. What kind of punishment is this? The guy on the farther T screams in desperation and pain. There aren't any people below us, except for a couple of Roman soldiers.

"Are you Jesus?" I ask the bearded man next to me.

"Jesus who?" answers the man.

"Jesus of Nazareth?"

"No, he was lucky. The crowd preferred him to me. I am Barabbas."

"Jesus Christ, you're Barabbas?"

"Yes, I am Barabbas. Pontius Pilate gave the crowd a choice between me and him. They chose him to be freed. And now I am hanging on this wretched pole."

I can't believe what I'm hearing. I even forget that I'm hanging on a wretched pole, too. Because, if Jesus isn't crucified and doesn't die today, what happens to Christianity? This is dire. I'm about to die in the most miserable way devised by man and destroy Christianity in the process. What did I do?

Wait, did I cause this? Saving Jesus is good, but I doubt that Christianity would spring forward without him being crucified. Oh God, perish the thought. But the crowd voted to let him go free; maybe his followers will multiply and Christianity will take place without him dying on the cross? Too many questions I can't answer, and I'm about to die.

"Barabbas, did you know Jesus Christ?" Then I remember, helped by the dumb look from Barabbas, that Jesus was not known in his time by the name of Christ. "I mean, Jesus of Nazareth?"

"You mean Jesus, the son of Joseph the carpenter?"

I nod.

"No, I only saw him when they brought us from the dungeons. That bastard Pilate offered us for a popular vote. I was assured that the crowd would be loaded with my sympathizers." He spits.

"Your sympathizers wouldn't be thieves, as well?"

He gives me a disgusted look. "What difference does it make? You win against the Roman scourge through any means." He spits again. "The Jews lost their appetite for freedom. They preferred the rabbi—"

"Hey, up there, shut up!" I hear a voice from down below. A Roman soldier looks at us sternly, forbidding Barabbas from bitching, which should be the right of any crucified man in the Roman Empire.

"So, what's your problem, Roman? Got a toothache?" says Barabbas, crossing his eyes. I have to say, he's either courageous or doesn't give a damn anymore.

"Don't anger him, Barabbas," says the other man on the cross, the other thief, I presume. This means that I'm a thief in this world. I'm one of the two thieves crucified with Jesus. Pathetic. I'm an insurance salesman!

"You think he might kill me?" Barabbas bursts into laughter.

The Roman soldier's not amused and, with his spear, he stabs Barabbas in his rib cage. Blood squirts out, not water. The Roman soldier is quick and moves out of the way before the blood can stain him.

"Is that the best you can do, Roman?" Barabbas is determined to provoke the soldier.

The soldier is angry now and moves his *pilum*, his spear, to strike Barabbas again.

"Halt, Livius!" shouts the other soldier, the officer in charge, maybe. "What do you think you're doing? If you kill the crucified, you'll be crucified yourself."

"The son of a bitch insulted me, Alerius," says the soldier Livius. He's enraged, shaking his pilum.

"Chicken!" yells Barabbas. "Donkey dung!"

Livius raises his pilum to strike, but Alerius steps in front of him. Barabbas continues insulting Livius and Alerius in so many colorful words that some of the insults' magnitude eludes me. The soldiers respond in kind, and that seems to defuse the hostility.

How did I cause this cataclysmic event, preventing Jesus from being crucified? Just by bumping into the second thief and taking his place? Or because the thief was free, and somehow he interfered with the fate of Jesus and Barabbas? I have mixed feelings. I've arrived at the wrong time and in the wrong place. I'm just an innocent crucifee! I can't imagine how I'm going to get out of this.

The exchange of savory words between Barabbas and Livius ends. Barabbas is catching his breath.

"Why am I crucified?" I ask innocently.

The other thief starts laughing. Alerius looks at me in surprise. "Because you're a thief. You stole."

"Why didn't you cut my hand off or flog me some more? Why crucify me for a petty crime?" I don't know where this is going; the soldiers won't understand this simple reasoning or have the power to get me off this lumber.

"You stole from the temple, you moron," says Alerius, as if he were talking to a dumb ass.

Oops! That's a major crime, and crucifixion is justifiable. But I didn't do anything. Is it me on this cross or the real thief? Maybe I only occupy his mind. I cannot see myself. "Hey, Barabbas!" I call on him.

Barabbas lifts his head and inhales deeply. He might be on the verge of passing out.

"What color is my hair?"

He looks dumbly at me. "Brown, black."

Why aren't I blonde? Everyone here has brown or black hair. "What color are my eyes?" I open my eyes wide for him to see.

He complies. "Brown."

Why don't I have blue eyes? Everyone has brown eyes in this part of the world. How can I find out who I am? Mirrors as I know them haven't been invented yet.

"Stop the chatter up there!" Livius shouts at us. "Would you listen to those two birds?" Livius says to Alerius. Alerius looks at me intently and with suspicion.

I see a possibility here. I bet Alerius suspects me of being homosexual, and at least this guy thinks it's a sin. Do they crucify homosexuals or stone them? Stoning is preferable, and I can get my hands free. "Barabbas, do you find me attractive?"

Barabbas's eyes open wide. "Go screw yourself, faggot."

The two soldiers are getting closer to my cross, paying more attention to me.

"How about you two – do you like me?" I move my hips as sensuously as the three nails holding me up allow.

Livius raises his pilum, but Alerius pushes it down. "You know what, Jew, if you're a faggot, you deserve to be yanked off the cross and stoned."

I make kissing gestures at Alerius. He raises his spear now but thinks better of it. "Livius, keep an eye on him. I need to talk to the centurion." As he says that he departs.

"Hey, Livius, I like you. Would you like to bend over for me?" I push my luck to the limit. Livius raises his pilum, pointing at my jewels. "Take it easy, big boy." I'm trembling now. This homophobe would castrate me without anesthetics.

"What the hell?" I hear the other thief exclaiming.

"Keep your mouth shut," I tell him. He could blow my bluff. This is a fine line I'm walking here. I'm trying to commute my death from painful and slow to painful and quick. I need my hands freed.

Hanging on the cross is killing me. I won't have to wait long. Alerius and the centurion arrive. The centurion, a burly man sweating profusely, carries his helmet in one hand. He has no spear. At least one less mad man with a sharp object, although he has a *gladius* at his side.

"Alerius, you've brought reinforcements. I hope you'll be gentle and not gang rape me." I hope I'm not overplaying my hand.

"Take this piece of shit down, off the pole," says the centurion. "We need to take him in the square and stone him." He turns to Alerius, who, along with Livius, is at the ready. "Good catch, soldiers. I would have hated to see him punished unjustly."

Thank God for righteous reasoning. After all, crucifixion is such a passive execution. It's like watching grass grow, although there wasn't any grass around this place. On the other hand, stoning is a team sport and an active execution. And there are plenty of stones littering the ground around here, unfortunately.

Alerius and Livius prepare to take me down. I hope they'll be careful and not hurt me in the process. Call me naïve, but that's not the case. The two brutes remove the stones at the base of the T's shaft. The T leans forward. I'm facing down, hanging from the spikes. Then, with a jerk, the pole leans some more. I can see the ants on the ground. I yell.

"Easy," says the centurion. "We don't want to kill him that fast and without other folks."

Good thinking, man! Falling on my face would ruin my acting career. Livius and Alerius each grab the ends of the cross beam and dragged the T out of the ground. They lower me and then drop me onto the dry, dusty, hard dirt. My nose breaks, and I'm bleeding. The darn wood beam knocks me on the back of the head. More pain. I should have stayed up there on the T. I don't have a chance to say good-bye to Barabbas and tell him that, thanks to me, he is hanging high and dry.

Livius and Alerius flip me over. Facing the sky, I can now breathe easier. My next worry is how they'll remove those awful spikes from my hands and feet. They unsheathe their short swords and start with my feet. I hope they won't amputate. I raise my head to watch, fearing what they may do.

Instead, very expertly, they use their two swords to pry the spike from the pole. The spike is still embedded in my feet. Livius, with total disregard for me, places the leather soul of his sandal on my legs and pulls the spike from my feet. Oh, God, it hurts. Blood is oozing from the wounds, and flies storm there for lunch.

They follow the same procedure for my hands and finally untie the ropes. Alerius pushes me off the T with his foot, and I roll over on my side. I'm off the T. It's a good day to pretend to be gay.

My hands are trembling, and I bring them up to my chin. Where is that calendar? Last time I found the map in the tunnel, I unfolded it, and I came back. If I don't find the calendar, I'll be hamburger meat.

To reinforce that thought, one of them, Livius, kicks me in the ribs and says, "Get up, swine."

I get up on my knees and elbows. I can't get to my feet. I have a hole in each one of them, from the instep to the sole. As I'm rising, my head lolls down, and, from my rags, from near my chest, the calendar drops onto the ground.

Please God, give me enough strength to grab and unfold this calendar and get the hell out of here. I lean on my head and pull my hands under my chest to reach for the calendar. A wisp of wind blows it away from me. Whatever blood I have left in me drains away. I'm as good as dead.

I rise up on my knees and watch the calendar fly away over the edge, down the steep hill. The three soldiers look at the piece of paper, not comprehending what it is. Once it falls over the edge, out of sight, they just shrug.

Holes in my feet, be damned. I need to get that calendar. I rise to my feet. They're on fire, and my knees are wobbly. I inhale and put the pain out of my mind. Quickly stepping on my heels, I walk to the edge and slide down the incline.

I tumble down, screaming in pain, and come to rest down at the bottom among a small avalanche of dirt and rocks. I'm on my back, head first, and I see the three soldiers laughing at me from the edge.

Where's the calendar? I roll over and search.

I've landed on it. Very gingerly, I pick it up, unfold it with as many fingers as I can muster motion in, and then I fold the calendar back.

Thank, God! I'm back in my office, holding the calendar in my intact hands. I place the calendar slowly on my desk, then I examine my hands, moving my fingers to make sure my piano playing isn't ruined. I'm good. There are no stigmata on my palms, either.

Next, I check my feet. I have beautiful feet, especially when they are hole-less. I stand up and have no pain. I am whole again.

What on Earth just happened? What's going on with this folding and unfolding stuff?

Then a thought occurs to me. Did I just alter history? I jump to my feet and look outside the window. What a relief! I can see the cross on St. Anthony's Church. I don't want to change history. I like the world just as it is. And, at least judging by the cross, Christianity still exists.

The experience I've just had was real, as real as I feel right now. Is all this happening in my head, or I am being transported into another universe? I think it is all in my head. But then, why did I feel all the pain I've just encountered? I'm physically OK now, but, psychologically, I'm not sure. Will I revisit these places in my nightmares? I'll worry about that tonight.

What do I do from now on? Should I stop handling any paper, folded or otherwise? And, you know, I'm alone here in my office at home. What if, days from now, they find only my shoes, while I am dead in another universe? I've had these experiences twice now, and the last one on the cross was pretty bad.

I check the wall clock; it's lunchtime. I wonder how much cash I have on me. I reach into my wallet and pull out a $10 bill and unfold it. Oh, no . . .

Chapter 3. Hell

"Achtung, achtung!" The voice booms from the speakers. I'm in a small train station. For the love of Jesus, what have I gotten myself into now? Swastika flags are waving in the wind everywhere. Am I in Nazi Germany?

The voice continues announcing the arrival of the next train. I'm pretty sure that the language is German, and I can understand it perfectly. It's an autumn day. Has the war started yet? It has to have. Judging by the signs, I'm in Nazi-occupied Poland. I need to find the date and year in this place. Ah, there is a newsstand.

Good old newspapers. They always display the date to show how fresh the news is, because tomorrow they'll wrap fish in them. And the date is September 6, 1943. The news in the paper is jubilant because German forces have stopped the Russian advance on the Eastern front and the Allies on the Italian Peninsula. As I'm reading the headlines, a man comes from behind the newsstand and gives me a shove that almost topples me over. Rough treatment for just gazing at the headlines!

Then his eyes get wider, and he points an accusatory finger at me. "*Jude*, Jew!"

All hell breaks loose. Before I can say a word, I'm surrounded by police and Wehrmacht soldiers. Seven guns are pointing at me.

I raise my hands. "What's the matter?"

"Where did you escape from, you dirty Jew?"

"What? I'm not a Jew," I speak honestly, but my legs are trembling.

"So what is this?" A soldier pokes me in the chest with his gun.

I look down and blanch. There it is, on my jacket, the yellow Star of David. I'm a Jew now, a Jew at the worst time for being a Jew. How will I get out of this predicament? If I tell them that I'm not a Jew, but an American, they will shoot me as a spy. For now I'm better off being a Jew, unless they shoot me for being a Jew. I'm in a no-win situation. I don't know what scares me more, being crucified by the Romans in the year thirty-something or being gassed by the Nazis in 1943.

"*Stabswachtmeister*, what shall we do with him?" the soldier asks the sergeant approaching us on the platform. By now many other people are sticking their heads out of the waiting room, watching the capture of a "dirty Jew." "Shall we shoot him behind the railroad tracks?" These men are definitely trigger-happy.

"Halt!" orders the sergeant. He scrutinizes me, and he's rather intrigued about my appearance. Everyone around me is skinny like a rail. War shortages tend to do that to civilians and soldiers alike. I, on the contrary, very seldom refuse to "super-size" my meal and look well-fed.

"It must be a mistake," I say. "I was drinking last night, and my buddies played a practical joke on me and sewed this patch on my jacket." I nod down at the Star of David. "I didn't know about this."

"Really?" says the sergeant. "Soldier, check for his papers."

The soldier who prodded me with his gun and volunteered to shoot me pro bono swings his gun over his shoulder and opens my jacket without bothering to unbutton it. Luckily, the coarse wool material opens without tearing off my buttons. He reaches in and pulls out a folded paper from my inner pocket, which he hands to the sergeant.

"Albert Kaufman," the sergeant reads the name on the paper. "You are registered as a Jew to be transported to Auschwitz on this morning's train. You bastard, you escaped from the train this morning. Well, there is another one coming through here in an hour. We'll load your ass on that one. Better late than never." He shows his teeth in a satisfied, cold smile.

This time I am as good as dead. I inherited some poor man's identity, and I have no way out except through Auschwitz. Just as I'm thinking that, one of the soldiers hits me in the back of my legs with the butt of his gun. I collapse. They order me to put my hands on my head and wait, while three soldiers keep guard with their guns pointed at me.

I don't have to wait long; even trains that transport Jews are punctual when Germans are involved. After the train stops and the sergeant has a talk with the officer in charge of the transport, they open one of the cattle cars' sliding doors and shove me inside. Next stop: Auschwitz.

It's unbearably crowded in the car, and it stinks. Many of the people have urinated or defecated on themselves. Men, women, and children are packed like animals to be taken to the abattoir. These people were removed quickly from the East as the front line was retreating west. I don't know if they are aware of their fate. They are scared, and they avoid my eyes. Someone like me placed in their car at this time in their journey could be an informant.

I carefully search all my pockets, looking for the $10 bill. The soldiers emptied my pockets more zealously while we waited for the train, but I'm hoping that somehow I'll find that bill in one of them. I don't. I'm dreading what's going to happen at the end of this ride into hell.

What to do? I wonder. Some of these people know or suspect the inevitable death that awaits them when they arrive at the camp. Many more are hoping that they are being taken to work camps. Why would the Nazis kill good workers? Sounds rational, but this is a world gone mad. Rationality died many years before.

I can inform them of the truth and start a riot when we arrive at the destination. For sure, there are more of us than guards, and in close proximity the guards can kill only so many of us before we can disarm and kill them. But will I be able to convince them that dying by fighting is better than dying like cattle? Am I able to change the herd mentality of scared people who hope that, as long as they do what they're told, their lives will be spared?

Well, I decide to follow my own advice: die fighting.

"Where are you from?" I finally ask. The people in this car are all Jews, mostly from Vinnytsya, Ukraine. Some speak German, some Ukrainian, others Polish, Russian, or Hebrew, but it doesn't matter because I can speak and understand all of them.

"Do you know what will happen to us when we arrive at Auschwitz?"

They don't know that the destination is Auschwitz. The news scares them. "We all will be gassed and our bodies incinerated." They look at me with horrified eyes. The women start crying.

"When we arrive there, we have two choices: walk to the gas chambers and die like sheep, or fight." This is not a fighting crowd. But

41

at least they know the outcome and their terrible options now.

One man approaches me and asks, "Do we have to fight? Can't we just run?"

"You can run, but each one will be caught and shot. We are better off fighting. Tell the rest what I said."

Throughout the journey, different people squeeze through to talk to me. In the end, most believe me and understand that death is inevitable. It's a matter of how it is going to happen.

We arrive in Auschwitz at night; it's raining lightly. The dark sky comes straight from hell. We are in the next-to-the-last car. The doors fling open, and the extermination camp's SS guards start shouting orders for us to get off and stand up for further instructions. Occasionally, a guard's German Shepherd barks, but otherwise it is quiet, aside from the noise the people make getting down from the car. Not far away, the crematorium fires illuminate the billowing smoke coming out of the chimneys.

We are upwind and don't smell the foul odor of burned human flesh.

The cars ahead of us have been emptied, and we can see, in the dim light of electric bulbs lining the path, the people ahead of us walking quietly to their deaths. Prison guards are cleaning and throwing dead bodies from the empty cars. Occasionally an SS guard would shoot the ones who were too weak to walk or too scared to get off. I look back in the car I occupied and see at least a dozen bodies lying dead inside.

Our group is getting ready to march to the gas chambers. There are several hundreds of us and only a dozen guards. Unfortunately, we are civilians, women and children, old and scared. The time to act is now. I may be an insurance salesman, but when it comes to dying, I get mean. "Jews!" I shout. "Remember Masada! We die on our terms! Attack the guards!"

It's a desperate act. We scatter in all directions. Half the people drop to the ground, frozen with fear, but many of us charge the nearest SS guards. The guards have automatic weapons and open fire into the crowd. A group of men and I are able to grab the gun of one guard, but one of their dogs bites my leg and drags me down. Bullets fly above me, mowing down the other standing men. The dog releases me, but two dead men are on top of me, pinning me down.

The SS guards are well trained, and they put down our desperate revolt quickly. Additional reinforcements arrive. They order the able-bodied prisoners to stand up against the cars. Sporadic gunfire can be heard in the distance, hunting down the ones who ran. The guards don't bother to capture and return any of those who ran – they just shoot them on the spot. The ground is littered with many bodies, dead or gravely wounded.

While the SS guards keep us at gunpoint, some of the other SS check to see who is still alive on the ground and then summarily shoot them. I'm certain that the rest of us will all be executed right here, standing against the cars. But we're not. Why waste bullets when poisonous gas is cheaper? After the situation is under control, the guards separate the men from the women and children.

The men are ordered back into one of the cars. The women and children are marched to the gas showers. I feel sick – not because we failed in our attempt, but because there is so much killing and carnage. We, the remaining men, are going to die as well. Death will arrive sooner for us than we thought it would, but not by poisonous gas. From the car the SS guards take us to a barracks, because the train has to leave to bring fresh cargo to the extermination camp.

The SS guards have a different plan for the remaining men. They have to teach a lesson to the new arrivals not to do what we've done. They hang one man from each light pole along the electrified fence near the railroad track, leading to the gates of the death camp. The SS guards make us watch. It is difficult to see one life at a time being snuffed out like a candle.

They run out of light poles by the time they get to me and four other men, and the guards are tired. They take us to join the latest group that's arrived, waiting their turn at the gas showers. Again, the women and children are separated from the men and taken to a different location.

Every hour, another train arrives, and the new captives are unloaded. It is a gruesome site

– desperate people with their meager belongings, walking silently, hoping that they will be sent to work as slaves and not killed. They are coming to the gates of hell, flanked by the train on one side and the hanged men on the light poles on the other.

I'm numb. What kind of nightmare have I sunk into? Or maybe I died and I am in hell. I've tried to be a hero, but the devil has won. I remember the $10 bill. Would I unfold it to escape from here, if I found it now? No, I want to stay here and die. God, living doesn't make sense anymore. Why am I here?

Why is anyone here? Why would Jews serve as a special detachment, called the *Sonderkommando*, helping the Nazis? These Jews are prisoners just as we are, dressed in striped "pajamas," and they are handling the grisly work of calming us down, asking us to undress, taking us to the shower chamber, and, after we are dead, removing our gold teeth and shoving our bodies into the crematorium. In a few months, they, too, will be killed, just like the ones they helped to the gas showers.

The SS guards hand off our group of men to the Sonderkommando. Surprisingly, these men in their striped outfits are calm and pleasant. They ask us to follow them to a barracks and to take our clothes off. They tell us we are going to be sanitized, showered, and deloused in the next room. Our clean clothes will be waiting on the other side of the shower room. We do as ordered and step into the "showers." Some believe what they are told; others want this whole thing to be over.

The doors are shut behind us, and I look expectantly at the showerheads on the ceiling. I've had a good life. I'm not married and didn't have any kids, so there's no one to take care of or to miss me much. If this is how it's going to end, so be it. Unless I'm already dead and this is hell, as I thought earlier. But I hope that I'm alive and that if I die I won't end up in a hell like this one.

Where does the gas come in, through the showerheads or other openings? I don't get the chance to observe the gassing because the man next to me hands me my folded $10 bill. I look at him. This is my ticket out of here. He is stoic. He doesn't know what he handed me.

I change my mind. I want to live. I unfold the bill and find myself sitting in my office, safe from hell. I've passed the stage of shock a long time ago. I just sit and stare at the wall. Whatever I experienced doesn't bother me. I'm resigned. Maybe I've transitioned mentally into the same state of mind as the Sonderkommando men, helping the devil and knowing that they, too, will be killed in the same fashion and not being bothered by it.

There's a bean burrito on my desk, which I don't remember buying. But then, who knows what I was really doing while I was experiencing the previous events? In spite of everything else, I'm hungry, so I eat it. The folded napkin is waiting for me to pick it up. No way! I wipe my mouth with the back of my hand.

The *National Geographic* is on top of a stack of magazines, and I open it to browse through it and get my mind off the terrible things I've just experienced. Something drops from the magazine, and I retrieve it from the floor. I look at it; it's a folded map of the moon. I throw it away, but it unfolds as it leaves my fingers.

I cringe.

Chapter 4. Red Luna

I find myself squeezed behind some light-frame aluminum seats, the kind I remember seeing on small airplanes. It smells like rubber in here. Through the crack between two of the chairs, I see two men in the seats, dressed in military green rubberized suits. Where the hell am I now?

"Telemetry kind of bothers me," says one voice from the seats. They're speaking Russian.

"What's happened?" asks another voice.

"We are deviating from our planned flight path," replies the first voice.

"I felt a jolt a few seconds ago," says a feminine voice.

"Something hit us?" asks the second man. "All indicators are normal, though."

"Sasha, we are deviating badly," says the woman. "My calculations show that we may not reach the moon."

What moon? Please make this some kind of simulator and not an actual space flight.

"Yakov, do we have any extra fuel to correct our position?" asks Sasha.

"Niet, no," comes the brusque answer from Yakov.

Over the speaker I hear, "This is ground control. Our telemetry shows that you're drifting. What's the situation, Captain?"

Ground control? I then realize that I'm weightless. I don't have much room to move, but I'm not lying on anything. I'm just floating in a tight space.

"This is the captain," says Sasha. "For some unknown reason we were knocked off course. Galina says she felt a jolt. Can you check to see if we had a close encounter with a meteor?"

"This is ground control. Did you say you were hit by a meteor?"

"Negative, ground control. Everything is normal in the capsule, but we are deviating from our course for an unknown reason. Could it have been a fly-by meteor?"

This is beyond crazy. I am in a Russian space capsule. Most likely I've affected the course of this mission. Should I say something?

"This is ground control. Negative – no meteors nearby. Repeat: no meteors nearby."

"What's going on, Sasha?" asks Yakov.

"The devil if I know," says Sasha. "We're heading away from the moon. Galina, do we have enough fuel in the ascent module to turn back?"

"Negative. Without the moon's gravitational break and assistance we cannot return, Sasha."

"Damn it!" shouts Sasha. "Ground control, we have an emergency on Krasnevoone. Repeat, emergency on Krasnevoone. We are deviating from the established course, and we will miss the rendezvous with the moon. This is an unknown cause, but we have slowed down. We need recommendations for corrective actions."

"This is ground control. Emergency declared. You have slowed down by 2%. We're searching for the cause and corrective actions. Stand by."

Yes, it is me, or my body, that's increased the mass of this space vehicle and slowed its velocity accordingly. What to do now? How can I get out of here and give these brave people a chance to return safely back to Mother Russia? I'm so apprehensive about this that I'm getting stomach cramps. Or maybe the burrito I ate was bad. Crap, I can't hold it any longer – I trumpet a long, noisy, and smelly fart.

The interior of the capsule isn't exactly quiet as a library. There are humming noises, buzzes, beeps, and ventilation fans, but my fart sounds like a bugle call. Loud and clear. I don't know if it's me, holding my breath and not moving, but the whole capsule becomes as quiet as a tomb.

"What was that?" Galina asks.

"Is that a gas leak?" says Yakov.

"Wow, it smells like beans," says Galina.

"Who farted?" Sasha asks bluntly.

"Not me," says Galina.

"Not me," says Yakov.

"Not me either," says an infuriated Sasha. "And there are only three of us in this tin can. God, the smell is bad! So one more time, *tovarish*: who farted?"

"Me," I say meekly from behind the seats.

A short monumental silence follows my confession, and then the scramble of three Russian cosmonauts trying to reach over the back of their seats to investigate the source of the voice begins. They create such a commotion that I'm sure the craft deviates even more from the already flawed course.

All three Russians are staring at me, as if they are seeing a ghost or an extraterrestrial. I'm frightened, too. And, at first, I can't tell who the woman is among them, because of their head bonnets.

"Who are you? What are you doing here?" thunders Sasha. He's the smallest of the three.

"S-s-sorry, I'm not sure how I got here." My bowels give up and release another fart. I'm sure it's Galina who retreats behind the seats with a disgusted scowl.

"What do you mean, you don't know how you got here?" Sasha says. He turns around. "Galina, change all radio contacts to the secure channel."

"Yes, Captain."

"Are you American?" Yakov asks. He's the biggest of them.

I nod, but have no idea how he knows that.

"Keep an eye on him," Sasha tells Yakov and retreats to his seat. "Ground control, this is Captain Mironov. Communicate only through the secure channel. Repeat, communicate only through the secure channel."

"This is ground control. Acknowledged. What's the problem, Captain?"

"I wouldn't tell them yet if I were you," I say from behind the seat.

"Shut up, you CIA spy," says Yakov, who punches me in the head.

I'm seeing stars. How brutal of him! I raise my hands above my head. "Let's talk first."

Sasha Mironov, the captain, overhears me. "Ground control, stand by." Galina takes over the conversation, delaying the response to ground control. "Talk," says Sasha, leaning over me from his seat.

"There's not much to say." I'm thinking hard about how to put this into words. "I woke up here a while ago. I don't know how I got here."

"Remember the jolt, Sasha?" interjects Galina.

"What do you mean you got here, while we've been in cosmos?" Sasha asks.

"Yes."

"How did you do that?"

"I don't know."

"What's your name? Who are you?"

"Hello, my name is Mike, and I am an insurance salesman."

Sasha and Yakov exchange dumbfounded looks. I wonder if they have insurance in the USSR.

"What year is this?" I ask. "The date?"

"1969," says Sasha gloomily.

"What's the date?"

"Why do you need to know the date?"

"Did *Apollo* land on the moon yet?"

Yakov hits me in the head again. "Talk, you imperialist pig!" He grabs me by the collar and pulls me up, easy to do in a weightless environment. But he pulls me so hard I fly over the backrests and land in Galina's lap. Or, I should say, I float into her lap. She squirms as if a rodent is trying to snuggle up to her bosom. I try to smile, but she doesn't reciprocate.

Here I am, I figure, in the front seat of a Soviet spacecraft going to the moon in 1969. Or, better yet, originally heading for the moon. Who knows where we are traveling now?

"I know that *Apollo 11* landed on the moon on July 20, 1969," I say defensively.

"What do you mean by 'landed,' as if it's already happened?" says Galina. "Today is July 4th."

"Our Independence Day? Oh shit! Where are we?" I ask.

"None of your business. How did you get here?" Yakov looks pissed; actually, I'd say he's more than pissed. I hope this capsule is anger-proof.

"OK, take it easy. I'm from the future."

"OK, future American man, tell us something from the future," says Sasha.

"I just told you – *Apollo 11* will land on the moon on July 20th, in 1969."

"You already said that. Something else," demands Yakov.

"What difference does it make what I tell you? You won't know the difference."

"Should I wring his neck?" Yakov says to Sasha.

"Are you crazy!" I object. "What do you think is going to happen to my corpse in here?"

"He's right," says Sasha. No wonder he's the captain. "We can't throw him out. Wait, maybe we can do it through the ascent module exit hatch."

I change my opinion about Sasha. "Killing me will not do you any good. Even if you eject my body from this craft, your trajectory has been altered. Your only salvation is to let me figure out how to return to my office."

"Your office?" Galina raises an eyebrow.

"Yes, that's where I was when I appeared here."

"When did you come from?" Sasha asks.

"2013."

"Forty-four years from now," comments Sasha. "Are we going to make it to the moon?" Sasha asks me.

"And return safely back to Earth?" adds Galina.

"Sorry, never heard of you guys making it that far." I should probably have said that with more understanding and compassion.

The three Russian cosmonauts exchange unsettled looks.

"Did you ever hear about this mission at all?" Sasha asks.

"Sorry, your country does not divulge its failures." I expect another pounding from Yakov, but he seems to be depressed. "I never knew that the USSR even attempted to land on the moon." More silence follows my demoralizing words. I observe the olive-green instrument panel cluttered with knobs, switches, blinking lights, a couple of small, old-fashioned TV screens, and mesh wire ovals for speakers. In the center of the panel, right in front of Yakov, there's the round cover of a manhole, the pressurized type.

"How do you suggest you get out of this predicament?" Sasha asks.

Did he say how *I* get out of this? I have news for you, Sasha: we're in this together, buddy. But then, there's no need to argue in such claustrophobic space. "I don't know. Something always comes up."

"Do you mean to say that you've done this before and gotten back?" Galina asks.

"What did you do to get here?" Sasha asks.

Even if I were to tell them, it is too unbelievable. Yakov would pound me some more to get me to tell the truth and nothing but the truth. "Look, I cannot explain this – it happens. I don't control it, either going or coming back."

"Don't lie! You are a CIA agent. You were placed in a big machine, and they transported you into our capsule to sabotage our mission." Yakov's nostrils flare like an enraged bull.

"I am no CIA agent. I am an insurance salesman. Besides, why send a man here? The CIA could have sent a sack of potatoes to screw up your flight."

Sasha raises his eyebrows and nods, kind of agreeing with me. Yakov doesn't seem convinced. Galina holds her head with one hand; she's either got a headache or she's thinking. I keep quiet.

"We need to contact ground control and tell them about this," Galina says.

"And tell them what? That we have an American onboard with us?" says Sasha.

"Well, yes," says Galina.

"This could start World War III. This could be proof that America is actively sabotaging our country's cosmos program," says Sasha.

"They wouldn't be that hotheaded," says Yakov, the cool head. "They'll talk, they'll figure things out."

"We can send images of him back to ground control," Galina suggests.

"You forgot, we don't have a camera on board. Remember, this mission was planned on a shoestring to save weight and to make it possible for us to reach the moon and return, if we got there. The only camera we have on this craft is the outside camera on the ascent module, so we can send proof back to Moscow that the Soviet Union's cosmonauts were the first to step on the moon. A quick walk, pick up some rocks, and then, hopefully, return home, followed by medals and a big parade in Red Square."

"Yes, you're right," agrees Yakov. "They cut corners to the max to make this mission possible and beat the Americans to the moon. Instead, we're going to join the others, floating in the cosmos forever."

Others? There were other accidents? There are Soviet cosmonauts floating in space? That thought chills me. I imagine space suits filled with mummified bodies or skeletons, in frozen and dead capsules. And soon I, along with these three, will share the same fate because of my foolish ability to provoke these events.

"There's not much we can do now," says Galina. "We need ground control's help. They'll figure something out. We must notify them."

"What if they don't believe us? They'll think we're crazy," says Sasha.

"Why are you so reluctant to inform ground control?"

"Go ahead, tell her," says Yakov.

"This spacecraft is rigged with explosives," admits Sasha.

"What! Why?" Galina shouts.

"In case of unexpected situations, the mission could be aborted by ground control."

"What kind of unexpected situations?" Galina asks.

"Well, you know." Sasha scratches his head. "For whatever reason and whenever ground control assesses that the mission is in danger –"

"Or potentially embarrassing for the Soviet Union," interrupts Yakov.

"This is crazy. Why haven't we been informed about this? I did not volunteer for an execution in the cosmos."

"It is on a need-to-know basis." Sasha looks uncomfortable.

"How come Yakov knew about this?"

"I deduced that possibility and later confirmed it with a friend who knew about it," says Yakov.

Galina is holding her head with both hands. I can't imagine what's going on in her mind. People can go crazy in situations like this. "I don't understand why ground control needs to kill us in case of a mishap," she says.

"It's the humane thing to do," says Sasha.

"Bullshit!" Galina screams.

"Have you guys considered defecting?" I've seen eyes pin me down before, but now I feel as if I'm being roasted alive by laser beams. "Well, you might be patriots, but Moscow must have considered the possibility of you landing in the USA. Accidentally or intentionally."

"We are here to serve the communist cause and our glorious country. We are expendable," says Yakov bitterly.

"That's right, tovarish," says a gloomy Sasha. "In any case, we'd better contact ground control. They'll blow us to smithereens if they don't hear back from us." Sasha reaches for the radio switch.

"It's all your fucking fault!" Galina explodes at me. Sasha doesn't flip the switch.

"I'm sorry. I didn't do it intentionally. I am in as much danger as you are. I at least don't have any cause to die for." I try to assure them with a crooked smile.

"The best thing would be for you to go back to where you came from," says Sasha.

Easier said than done. But wait: the last thing I did before all this happened was unfold the map of the moon, or, kind of unfold it. "Alright, let me tell you what I did before I got here." They all look up with hope. "I unfolded a map of the moon." Now they look at me with doubt.

"What kind of bullshit is that?" scowls Yakov.

"That's all that I do, and then I appear some place I cannot possibly imagine or want to be. To return, the same piece of folded paper somehow appears in my hands, and then I fold it back, and I return."

"Where else have you been?" Galina inquires.

"No time for stories," interrupts Sasha. "Let him figure how to get out of here."

"Even if he gets out of here, we're still screwed," says Yakov. "He lives, we die."

"Have you considered the possibility that the mass of my body disappearing might affect your flight path in a beneficial way?"

"That makes sense," agrees Sasha. "Then do something. Do your thing." He gestures with his hands as if to hurry me along.

"Do you have a map of the moon on board?" I ask.

"Not here but in the ascending module," says Sasha. "Let's go. Galina, pressurize the cabin in the landing module."

"*Da*," she replies, and, after a moment, "The pressure is equalized."

Sasha nudges Yakov to unlatch the manhole. That's the hatch to get into the ascending module.

Yakov unlatches the cover by turning four captive thumbscrews. There's a thin hiss of air as Yakov opens the hatch, which swings in on tiny hinges. "There you are."

"I'll go in first," says Sasha. "Yakov, shove Mike in after me."

Although Sasha calls me by my name, it sounds as if he's referring to me as cargo.

It takes about two minutes for Sasha to contort and squeeze through the opening. He goes in feet first. Then it's my turn. Yakov pushes me in head first, like a rolled carpet. Although I'm weightless, it takes considerable exertion on my part to squeeze through. I have to make the effort to move forward, followed by the effort to stop. There isn't a great distance to cover in entering the ascending module, but I have to go through a lot of pushes, pulls, and stops. It takes me five minutes to enter the cabin.

If the capsule above is small, this cabin was built for a woman and a boy. Maybe it was designed for Sasha and Galina.

Sasha and I are now nose to nose, feeling each other's breath. "What do you need, again?" he asks.

"The map."

"Let me see. It is stored in this kit." Sasha unzips a side compartment and pulls out a plastic bag. He opens it and retrieves a folded document, a black and white map of the moon. "Here – do what you need to do."

I take the map and unfold it. Nothing happens. I fold it back; nothing happens. I repeat the folding and unfolding several times, but nothing. I even fold it and unfold it the wrong way, but still nothing. "I can't explain it. It doesn't seem to work."

"I can see that. Is this some kind of delaying tactic?"

"What do you mean?"

"Are you delaying and distracting us until you Americans capture this craft?"

"No such thing. Have you looked outside through the portholes? Do you see any American crafts nearby?"

"No, but being busy with you I haven't had a chance to look outside." He turns sideways and looks out through one of the round portholes.

I do the same thing with the porthole on my side. Wow, it's my first time in space, and I get to look outside. It's pitch black. The sun is shining in at a slant angle on the window, and the glare obscures any starlight. Totally disappointing.

Sasha pushes me aside, and I figure he wants to look out through the porthole I'm peering through. I look out through his porthole, and I see Earth – it's a half disk, blue with white whiffs of clouds. Lo and behold, I see the moon, too; it's a half-moon and much bigger than I could ever see it from Earth. Wow!

"I don't see anything, but all possibilities are on the table," says Sasha. "Try again."

I fiddle with the map. It's a Russian moon map, so it doesn't work. I am sure it has to be my map, not just any map. "It's not working," I say, defeated.

Sasha frowns and looks at me in silence for a long time. "Well, now you got to see the interior of the ascending module as well. Are you satisfied?"

As a matter of fact, now that he mentions it, I hadn't noticed this cramped space before. It's lit by a five-volt light, and I can barely make out any details other than switches and dead lights, a small TV screen, and stuff I can't comprehend at all. "I told you, I am an insurance salesman, not a spy. I have no idea what I'm looking at."

"I saw you how you looked at the control panel in the capsule."

"I'm not a spy." I try to spread my arms out, to show my innocence, but the space is small.

"As a matter of fact, we never searched you." Sasha frisks me, taking advantage of my partly spread arms. He does a decent job of finding

69

nothing. I have a blue jumper on, but even if I had my own clothes on me, when I am in the office I leave my keys and wallet in a drawer. My pockets are empty.

"Nothing, no ID, nothing," says Sasha. He's disappointed, but now he's more suspicious. Spies carry false IDs or no IDs at all. To him, I'm the no-ID spy.

"Look, I don't carry anything in my pockets when I'm in my office. Do you have an ID with you?"

He looks surprised at my question, then he points to his name above his left pocket on his suit. "I'm on a mission. I don't need ID. And I think you are on a mission, and you don't need ID, either." He's dead serious.

"Look, I don't know how to explain this, but I wasn't sent on any sabotage mission. It just happened."

He quickly grabs me by the collar, rubbing the fabric between his fingers as if trying to detect concealed cyanide capsules. There's nothing in my collar. "Do you realize what will happen when four people are drifting in a can in the empty cosmos?"

"I don't want to imagine it," I say earnestly. "But, tell me, how come you can't maneuver back on course, or return?"

"We don't have enough fuel."

"You must have enough fuel to land on the moon."

Sasha smiles bitterly. "We don't have a Saturn rocket, like you Americans. We had to send two rockets to the moon – one with us and the ascending module, which is what we will use to come back from the surface of the moon. The other rocket contains the landing module and fuel to land and return home. The fuel is there." He points somewhere out where the moon might be. "When we arrive at the moon, we'll use its gravity to slow down and orbit it, couple with the landing module and the fuel, and we would be in business, as you Americans say."

Even I, an insurance salesman, realize what a stupid plan this is. And we are the proof.

"The brilliant people back home never considered the possibility that we may not get to the moon, and therefore never return home." Sasha looks at me with a sour face.

He pushes me toward the open hatch, out of the ascending module's cabin. I float to the opening and grab the rim, pulling myself into the capsule. I stop, my head sticking up through the opening. I can't believe my eyes.

Yakov is between Galina's legs, rhythmically moving his space suit buttocks between her spread legs. Her boots are planted on the dashboard. She responds in rhythm to Yakov's movements. They are both moaning with pleasure. For crying out loud, they're screwing! In their space suits? I guess it's possible, judging by their interaction.

I don't pay attention to how long it takes or even how I get back into the capsule while staring at the finest Soviet cosmonauts having intercourse in space. I wonder if the capsule is rocking. It doesn't matter – there is no one to come knocking. But my reverie is shattered when I hear Sasha shouting, "What the hell are you doing? You're acting like two peasants!"

I don't know why he calls them peasants. I suppose in Russia only peasants screw wantonly. Yakov and Galina turn bright red and push away from each other. I can hear the sound of zippers closing the front-bottom access on their suits. I have to admit that the Soviet Union can claim another first – sex in space. Would they call them cosmofuckers?

I'm pushed aside as Sasha squeezes back into the capsule. I end up crammed between Yakov and Sasha. Galina is looking the other way, through the porthole. I bet she never did this before. I mean in space. Yakov is breathing heavily from the effort.

"What were you thinking?" screams Sasha.

"Hell, we're going to die anyway. What difference does it make?" Yakov is defensive.

"Wait until I tell your mother about this, Galina," says Sasha in a huff, shaking a finger at her.

"Thank you for not telling my husband," she snorts sarcastically. She gets the evil eye from Sasha. She turns back and looks through the porthole, chewing on a fingernail.

We all sit/float quietly for some time to recover from the shock and elevated blood pressure for some. The lights on the dashboard are blinking furiously. Ground control has been trying to reach the spacecraft, but no one has responded.

"It didn't work." Sasha finally breaks the silence. "We have no use for him."

My eyes get wide. Soviet cosmonauts are military people. They are soldiers first.

The three act as one. Sasha holds my legs, Galina holds my arms at the wrists, and Yakov – the brute – grabs me by the neck. Fuck! These assholes are about to kill me!

I struggle and somehow I manage to rotate and face Yakov. Bad idea, because now he has his thumbs on my Adam's apple. I try to get away from his hands. We are a ball of arms, bodies, and legs in the space of a bathtub.

I manage to reach one of Yakov's hands and bite him on the finger. I hear the cracking of a finger bone, and Yakov howls. I end up with my face against the seat, the others on top of me, or under me – in space, you can't tell.

In our struggle, we must have pushed open a lot of switches, because there's a cacophony of voices calling in, buzzers, blinking lights, and sirens. Ground control is most likely listening, and they're thinking the crew has gone mad. I wonder how far from the kill switch is the finger of a high-ranking tovarish down in the Kremlin.

Then I see it. The map is stuck between the seats. I move my head and pull my hands to my mouth to release Galina's grasp. The bitch has long fingernails. I bite her hands. Quick bites, bitter bites so she will free me. She lets me go. I kick at Sasha and crawl closer to the map.

I pull it out and unfold it . . .

Chapter 5. Reality

I'm back in my office. I inhale with pleasure. The air is sweet and plentiful, not like the rubberized, rotten-cabbage, bean-farts-smelling air in the capsule. But wait: I am safe, but the cosmonauts will die. I feel sorry for them, despite the fact that they were trying to kill me. What choice did they have? They wanted to live as well. I basically killed them. I'm depressed. Everywhere I go I cause pain and death.

I see the napkin on the desk. I cannot do this again. Or, just do it and don't return. I grab the napkin and unfold it.

I look up and see dunes of yellow-beige sand opening before my eyes. They go on forever. The sky is the same deep blue, without a cloud. Yes, it's the Sahara desert. Why am I back here?

From my left side two Bedouins walk by me, pushing a lawn mower. A gasoline powered, red lawn mower. They don't mind me and continue walking away.

"Hold it, fellows!" I shout at them.

They stop and look at me crookedly. One of them asks, "Who are you?"

"I'm Mike, the insurance salesman from America." I cross my arms and pump my chest, as if I'm an action hero.

"You're American?"

"Yes. What are you doing with that lawn mower?" I point an accusatory finger at it. I'm looking for trouble.

"We had it fixed," says the other.

"What for? To mow sand?"

"No. To mow Americans," says the first Bedouin, the one who's pushing the lawn mower.

I swallow hard. I didn't expect that answer.

Without saying another word, he pulls the cord, starts the mower, and pushes the lever into high gear.

Dumb shits! The lawn mower does not have a grass catcher, the exhaust door opens, and the mower becomes a sand blower. They get blasted. They cough, rub their eyes, and roll down the dune. I stop the mower with a satisfied smile.

The dogsled appears in the distance. This scene is repeating. What the heck is going on? I move the lawn mower and bar the sled's path.

The woman dressed in the black burkha riding on the back rails calls to the dogs and stops the sled right in front of me. The Arab man dressed in the pinstriped, dark suit stands up and steps out of the sled. His shiny shoes sink into the desert sand. He removes his mirrored sunglasses. I can see his eyes, they are light blue.

"Hello," he says in perfect English, as he places his glasses in his top pocket.

"H-hello," I manage to say.

"How are you doing?"

I recover from my verbal stumbling. "What's going on here?"

"You tell me," he says plainly.

"You do know what's happening." I point an accusatory finger at him.

"Of course. All of us do."

"All of you? How many are you? Who are you?"

"We are your creation," he says with a smile.

"Bull! My creation?"

"Yes. It all comes from here." He points to my forehead. I bend slightly backward, afraid of his touch. We eye each other. "Yes, you made us. In your mind, once you discovered how to fold or unfold reality."

"I made all this up, even the cosmofuckers?"

"You did."

"When I fold a piece of paper, I unfold a new reality?"

"Yes. And it is your doing alone."

"Were all those other realities real?"

"Just as real as I am."

I grab his shoulder. Yes, he's real. "I caused the death of so many people because of my imagination?"

"True. Just as you are someone else's imagination, and he may kill you."

"Are you saying that nothing is real? It's all just our imagination?"

"That's the only reality."

"What do you mean, he may kill me?"

"Or she, or it, or they may kill you. You imagine that death is the end and create a reality of ending, but it is not the end. Imagination, reality, death, and all other happenings are real and are not, at the same time."

"How do I stop these too-real-to-be true realities I encounter?"

"Very simple. You already know the answer." He makes a gesture to the woman on the sled rails. She removes her burkha.

She's the young woman in the baby-blue outfit from the indigo-blue room.

"I Often Wonder," I say.

The End

Thank you for reading my book. If you enjoyed it and would like to help other readers with your comments please write a review on Amazon. And of course I much appreciate your review as well. Amazon book link.

For more information about my books please visit sandru.com/blog/

Or visit me at my website: sandru.com and subscribe to my mailing list.

(Your e-mail will not be sold or used for spam)

Other Books by Dumitru (Mit, DG) Sandru

Science Fiction

Sferogyls (Timurud Book 1) by Mit Sandru

The Maggotroll Empire invades the Sferogyls' planet. The Sferogyls are unarmed and have no defense against the imperial battleships. The gods resurrect Timurud and send him to help the peaceful Sferogyls fight the invaders. Will the Sferogyls win the war in space and defend their planet, or perish?

Gold Rush Mystery (Terraspantion Chronicles, Bk. 1) by Mit Sandru.

America is back on the Moon, and we intend to stay and establish a self-sustaining permanent base for tourism and mining. The work is challenging, the environment is deadly, but the astronauts Mia, Geo and Roby succeed in building the moon base, even if they landed in a mysterious crater.

Time Hole, (Terraspantion Chronicles, Bk. 2) by Mit Sandru.

Mining on the moon is a hazardous affair. Deedee and Arno, two lunar generalists, find perils beyond what they signed up for when they travel on the lunar surface at night . . . on the dark side of the Moon. Time will not be the same after they fall into the Time Hole.

Teen, Children Fantasy

Arboregal, the Lorn Tree, by D.G. Sandru.

YouTube: https://bit.ly/2OtDj5c

Four youngsters, Melissa, Perry, Nathan and Michelle materialize in a desolate world where giant, mile-high trees, support all life. They find shelter in the Lorn Tree among the Lorns. Soon after they discover that an evil spirit, Hellferata, wants them dead. Fearful Lorns want to expel the youngsters from their tree, which would be a dead sentence since monsters roam the land at night.

Will their ingenuity, cunning, and courage help them escape, or will Hellferata mete out her wrath before they can escape?

Paranormal, Mystery, Thriller

The Pregnant Pope (Book 1 TIO Series), by Mit Sandru.

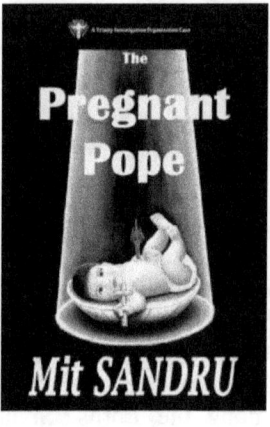

The 92-year-old Pope is pregnant. He hasn't undergone any medical procedures, but he carries a fetus in his abdomen. Is this a case of self-cloning, or a mutation? Is this an Immaculate Conception, or Satan's work? Find out how Claire, Travis, and Prescott solve this mystery and the bizarre outcome.

The Devolution of Adam and Eve (Book 2 TIO Series) by Mit Sandru

A pandemic causes billions of people to lose their minds. The world's government health agencies cannot identify the pathogen and develop an antidote. It comes from another realm, and only Claire, Prescott, and Travis can solve this enigma. Will they prevent the end of humanity before it's too late?

Vampires - Thriller & Romance

YouTube: https://bit.ly/2pahMDI

YouTube: https://bit.ly/2lPwAt4

Vampire (Vlad V, Bk 1) by Mit Sandru.

Meeting a vampire isn't something that happens every night, even on the New York City subway. But never in her wildest dreams did Cat Sanders ever expect to meet the vampire Vlad V Draculesti and survive the encounter. Instead, she became his confidant. Why was she so lucky?

R.I.P., The Death of a Vampire (Vlad V, Bk 2) by Mit Sandru.

Vlad V Draculesti is dying because of an incident that happened decades ago. Unfortunately for Vlad V, the US intelligence agencies investigate him to find out his true identity, and centuries old life. Will Cat Sanders and vampire friends be able to help him die in peace, or will Vlad be discovered for being a vampire and die in a US Federal research laboratory?

Vampire Slayers (Vlad V, Bk 3) by Mit Sandru.

Cat Sanders is a billionaire, but not all is well. Her nemesis, Veronica Seyler, allied with a vampire-slayer drug cult, demands extortion money or she will be killed.

Cat's vampire friend, Angelique, comes to her aid. But the cult is more cunning and dangerous than even her vampire friend could handle. Would Cat and Angelique be able to come out of this alive even if Cat pays the ransom?

Vampires of Transylvania (Vlad V, Bk 4) by Mit Sandru

Cat Sanders has a simple task: spread Vlad V's ashes in Transylvania at midnight, during full moon. But in Transylvania Vlad V has centuries old enemies who take her and her friend Tudor hostage, placing them in iron cages among zombies and proto-vampires. Will they be able to escape from the blood sucking proto-vampires and flesh-eating zombies, or become zombies themselves?

The Queen of Vampires: A New Queen Arises (Vlad V, Bk 5) by Mit Sandru

The Vampire Queen, Eleonore von Schwarzenberg, is bloodthirsty and vengeful on Cat Sanders and her friends. She plans the most painful death for them. Cat and her friends find themselves entrapped and helpless to avoid her wrath.

Will Cat and her friends be able to escape and survive the Queen of Vampires' fury?

Non-Fiction, Political

Escape from Communism, by Dumitru Sandru, a True Story and Commentary.

Life under communism is cruel and inhumane. Commit the smallest political infraction, and the secret police will arrest you. The only ray of hope is the West, but it is a crime to escape by crossing the border illegally, and anyone caught is beaten and imprisoned, sometimes even shot. This is my story of what happened and how I reached freedom.

Coloring Book

Abstract Dreams: Coloring Book 1 (Sandru's Art) by Dumitru Sandru

YouTube: **https://bit.ly/2Ulc9RT**

Reward your soul with the smooth and pleasing lines of Abstract Dreams

https://www.sandru.com/Coloring.html

T-Shirts and other stuff:

https://www.zazzle.com/store/dgsandru/products

Visit my e-Gallery at:

https://www.sandru.com/SferogylsArt.html

https://www.sandru.com/LornTreeArt.html

http://dumitru-sandru.artistwebsites.com/

https://www.pinterest.com/mitsandru/

About Dumitru "Mit" Sandru

Mit Sandru was born in the greater area of Transylvania in the last millennium; make that last century since he's not a vampire. Yet. When he was six years old, a soldier shot him at point blank range with a Kalashnikov. He survived. He outsmarted his German teacher, and survived a tornado in the middle of a wheat field. Not concurrently. When he was 18 years old, he escaped from a country resembling a concentration camp, luckily without being killed. He outran mean border patrol dogs in a foreign country, in the darkness of night, while jumping over six-foot tall stonewalls. Superman he's not. He came to the USA in search of freedom, glory, wealth, and fame. He's still searching for three of those. Lightning grazed him, and he caught a shark by the tail. Once. A monkey attacked him in Japan, but his daughter saved him. He avoided many rattlesnake bites, and built a house. No relation between the snakes and the house. Life eventually tamed him and he became a responsible citizen, with a wife, two daughters, dog and cat. And lately two grandsons. The taming part is questionable. He acquired an engineering and management degree and attempted to acquire other degrees in music, marketing, and IT. A certified student he is. He obtained many professional licenses, which he hardly used, but looked good on his wall. At 59-¾ years old he quit the corporate life and a six-figure salary. Rumor has it that he was given the golden handshake. He was finally free to pursue his dreams of writing, painting and music. During his professional life he painted hundreds of canvases, and composed dozens of tunes, while since his golden handshake he wrote 14 books; although one is a coloring book. And that was in just the first half of his life.

Disclaimer: Everything written here is true, but the bullets were blanks.

I am Mit Sandru and I approve this unabashed bio.

Want to see and read more about the second half of his life?

Webpage: http://sandru.com

Twitter: http://bit.ly/1kVzh6Z

Facebook: http://on.fb.me/1OiYOCn

Goodreads: http://bit.ly/1TgVbNa

Amazon: Amzn.to/1UtpTFR

Pinterest: https://www.pinterest.com/mitsandru/

YouTube videos

Arboregal, The Lorn Tree:

https://bit.ly/2OtDj5c

Abstract Dreams: Coloring Book 1:

https://bit.ly/2Ulc9RT

Vlad V Vampire Series:

https://bit.ly/2pahMDI

Lucy the Vampire Dog:

https://bit.ly/2lPwAt4

www.ingramcontent.com/pod-product-compliance
Lightning Source LLC
Chambersburg PA
CBHW071339130626
46556CB00004B/1954